W9-CAV-951

by Margaret Hillert
Illustrated by Kinuko Craft

WHAT IS IT?

by Margaret Hillert
Illustrated by Kinuko Craft

DEAR CAREGIVER, The *Beginning-to-Read* series is a carefully written collection of classic readers you may remember from your own childhood. Each book features text comprised of common sight words to provide your child ample practice reading the words that appear most frequently in written text. The many additional details in the pictures enhance the story and offer the opportunity for you to help your child expand oral language and develop comprehension.

Begin by reading the story to your child, followed by letting him or her read familiar words and soon your child will be able to read the story independently. At each step of the way, be sure to praise your reader's efforts to build his or her confidence as an independent reader. Discuss the pictures and encourage your child to make connections between the story and his or her own life. At the end of the story, you will find reading activities and a word list that will help your child practice and strengthen beginning reading skills.

Above all, the most important part of the reading experience is to have fun and enjoy it!

Shannon Cannon

Shannon Cannon,
Literacy Consultant

Norwood House Press • P.O. Box 316598 • Chicago, Illinois 60631
For more information about Norwood House Press please visit our website at
www.norwoodhousepress.com or call 866-565-2900.

LIBRARY OF CONGRESS CATALOGING-IN-PUBLICATION DATA
Hillert, Margaret.
  What is it? / Margaret Hillert ; Illustrated by Kinuko Craft. — Rev. and expanded library ed.
    p. cm. — (Beginning-to-read series)
    Summary: "A curious red string leads two youngsters to an unusual playmate"—Provided by publisher.
    ISBN-13: 978-1-59953-154-0 (library edition : alk. paper)
    ISBN-10: 1-59953-154-2 (library edition : alk. paper) [1. Stories in rhyme.] I. Craft, Kinuko, ill. II. Title.
    PZ8.3.H554Wh 2008
    [E]—dc22   2007035275

Beginning-to-Read series (c) 2009 by Margaret Hillert.
Library edition published by permission of Pearson Education, Inc. in arrangement with Norwood House Press, Inc. All rights reserved.
This book was originally published by Follett Publishing Company in 1978.

What is it? What is it?
Oh, what do I see?
Something little and red.
Go get it for me.

7

Can you guess what it is?
Can you get it? Oh, no.

For look at it. Look at it.
Look at it go!

But where is it now?
And what will it do?

I see it. I see it.
Do you see it, too?

My little dog helps us.
He likes to have fun.

He can play. He can jump.
He can run, run, run.

I guess it is here.
It is here in this spot.

And now we will get it.
Oh, no, we will not!

And look at it now.
Here it is, where we play.

This little red something
Will not get away.

Now where will it go?
And what can we do?

I see it. I see it.
I see Mother, too.

Down, down it can go.
Down, down it can run.

We like this. We like this.
We like to have fun.

It is fun to play here.
Jump in. One, two, three.

I see it. Go get it.
Go get it for me.

Look here, now. Look here, now.
Look here at this car.

And guess what we see now?
We see where you are.

We see you. We see you.
Oh, you are the one!

Come play with us now.
We can play and have fun.

The following activities support the findings of the National Reading Panel that determined the most effective components for reading instruction are: Phonemic Awareness, Phonics, Vocabulary, Fluency, and Text Comprehension.

Phonemic Awareness: Rhyming Words

1. Reread the story aloud without showing the pages. Pause on every page spread and ask your child to tell you which two words rhyme:

p. 7: see/me	pp. 14-15: spot/not	pp. 22-23: three/me
pp.8-9: no/go	pp. 16-17: play/away	pp. 24-25 car/are
pp. 10-11: do/too	pp. 18-19: do/too	pp. 26-27: one/fun
pp. 12-13: fun/run	pp. 20-21: run/fun	

Phonics: Rhyming Words

1. Fold a piece of paper lengthwise and draw a line on the fold to divide the paper into two columns.

2. Write the following list of words in the first column: no, spot, car, do, see, play, one.

3. Write the following list of words in the second column: fun, too, go, away, are, not, three.

4. Ask your child to read each list of words.

5. Ask your child to draw a line from each word in the first column to the corresponding rhyming word in the second column.

Vocabulary: Movement Words

1. Write the following words on index cards and point to them as you read them to your child:

   follow   climb   slide   row   drive

2. Mix the words up. Say each word in random order and ask your child to point to the correct word as you say it.

3. Mix the words up and ask your child to read as many as he or she can.

4. Say the following sentences aloud and ask your child to point to the word that is described:

   - The little people _____ the red string. (follow)
   - They _____ the long staircase with the dog. (climb)
   - They _____ down from the city to get to the canoe. (slide)
   - The little people _____ the canoe across the water. (row)
   - They _____ the dragon car to find the cat playing with the string. (drive)

Fluency: Echo Reading

1. Reread the story to your child at least two more times while your child tracks the print by running a finger under the words as they are read. Ask your child to read the words he or she knows with you.

2. Reread the story, stopping after each sentence or page to allow your child to read (echo) what you have read. Repeat echo reading and let your child take the lead.

Text Comprehension: Discussion Time

1. Ask your child to retell the sequence of events in the story.

2. To check comprehension, ask your child the following questions:

   - Is this story real? How can you tell?
   - How did the little people get from the floating city to the boat?
   - What is your favorite part of the story? Why?
   - What parts of the story could happen in real life?

WORD LIST

What Is It? uses the 55 words listed below.

This list can be used to practice reading the words that appear in the text. You may wish to write the words on index cards and use them to help your child build automatic word recognition. Regular practice with these words will enhance your child's fluency in reading connected text.

and	get	me	the
are	go	mother	this
at	guess	my	three
away			to
	have	no	too
but	he	not	two
	help(s)	now	
can	here		us
car		oh	
come	I	one	we
	in		what
do	is	play	where
dog	it		will
down		red	with
	jump	run	
for			you
fun	like(s)	see	
	little	something	
	look	spot	

ABOUT THE AUTHOR Margaret Hillert has written over 80 books for children who are just learning to read. Her books have been translated into many different languages and over a million children throughout the world have read her books. She first started writing poetry as a child and has continued to write for children and adults throughout her life. A first grade teacher for 34 years, Margaret is now retired from teaching and lives in Michigan where she likes to write, take walks in the morning, and care for her three cats.

Photograph by Glenna Washburn

ABOUT THE ADVISER Shannon Cannon contributed the activities pages that appear in this book. Shannon serves as a literacy consultant and provides staff development to help improve reading instruction. She is a frequent presenter at educational conferences and workshops. Prior to this she worked as an elementary school teacher and as president of a curriculum publishing company.